West Goshen School Library

WITHDRAWN

P9-CRE-268

. . . for parents and teachers

Everyone gets angry sometimes. Anger is a natural reaction to things we dislike.

As young children, we could be open and natural in expressing our anger and hostility. However, we were also taught from a very early age always "to be nice." As we grow up, expressing anger, especially to persons with whom we are upset, becomes increasingly difficult.

Sometimes I Get So Mad is a story that carefully traces a childhood argument and its resolution. I feel certain that the use of this story will encourage deeper understanding of personal attitudes. In facilitating positive expression of negative emotions, it may enhance the quality of many relationships. I encourage parents and professionals to consider integrating this material into their personal, educational, or professional contacts with young children.

MANUEL S. SILVERMAN, Ph.D.
ASSOCIATE PROFESSOR AND CHAIR
DEPARTMENT OF GUIDANCE AND
   COUNSELING
LOYOLA UNIVERSITY OF CHICAGO

Copyright © 1980, Raintree Publishers Inc.

All rights reserved. No part of this book may be
reproduced or utilized in any form or by any means,
electronic or mechanical, including photocopying,
recording, or by any information storage and retrieval
system, without permission in writing from the Publisher.
Inquiries should be addressed to Raintree Childrens Books,
205 West Highland Avenue, Milwaukee, Wisconsin 53203.

Library of Congress Number: 79-24057

1 2 3 4 5 6 7 8 9 0 84 83 82 81 80

Printed in the United States of America.

Library of Congress Cataloging in Publication Data

Hogan, Paula Z
  Sometimes I get so mad.

  SUMMARY: Karen expresses her anger in passive,
negative ways until she sees what can happen when
she deals with it directly and positively.
  [1. Anger — Fiction] I. Shapiro, Karen.
II. Title.
PZ7.H68313Sm   [Fic]   79-24057
ISBN 0-8172-1359-7 lib. bdg.

West Goshen School Library

SOMETIMES
I GET
SO MAD

F
Hog
9-80
4535

by Paula Z. Hogan

illustrated by Karen Shapiro

introduction by Manuel S. Silverman, Ph.D.

RAINTREE CHILDRENS BOOKS
Milwaukee • Toronto • Melbourne • London

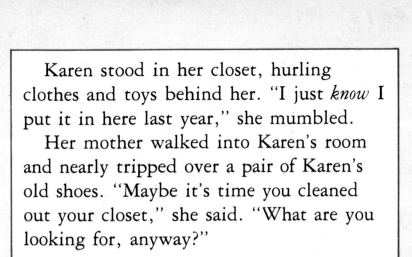

Karen stood in her closet, hurling clothes and toys behind her. "I just *know* I put it in here last year," she mumbled.

Her mother walked into Karen's room and nearly tripped over a pair of Karen's old shoes. "Maybe it's time you cleaned out your closet," she said. "What are you looking for, anyway?"

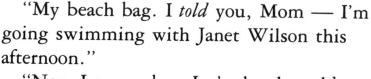

"My beach bag. I *told* you, Mom — I'm going swimming with Janet Wilson this afternoon."

"Now I remember. Isn't she that older girl who lives down the street?"

Before Karen could answer, her mother added, "I remember something else. *I* told *you* that I had to work this afternoon. That means you'll have to take your sister along with you to the beach."

Karen pulled her beach bag out from under a pile of books. "Rosie's just a little kid," she groaned. "What will Janet think? Oh, this is going to ruin the whole day!"

"Only if you let it," said Karen's mother. "Rosie can't come to the office with me, and she can't be left alone here. So you can either take her along to the beach or stay home with her — take your pick."

Minutes later, Karen and Rosie were walking toward Janet's apartment building.

"When we get to the beach, will you help me build a sand castle?" Rosie asked.

"Don't be such a pest," answered Karen. "I'm too big for sand castles."

7

Janet was waiting on her porch. "Hi, Karen. You didn't tell me you were bringing your little sister along."

Karen linked arms with Janet. "Don't worry," she said. "Rosie will keep out of our way." Over her shoulder she called, "Won't you, Rosie?"

It was a short walk to the beach. Karen and Janet dropped their bags and dashed across the sand and into the water. Rosie stayed behind and played on shore.

"Let's swim out past the white marker," said Janet after a while. "It's nice and deep out there."

Karen floated on her back. "We'd better not, Janet. We might get into trouble."

"Sounds like you're scared," Janet teased.

"No, I just like it right here," said Karen. "Anyway, I'm getting hungry. Do you want some of my cookies?"

"I sure do!" said Janet, splashing toward shore. "Come on, I'll race you."

Just as the girls were finishing their cookies they heard someone calling, "Hey, Janet! Janet, over here!"

A tall girl was running toward them.

Janet waved her hands. "Patty!" she shouted. "I can't believe it — what are you doing here?"

"I'm building a snowman," Patty teased. "What's it look like I'm doing?"

"You know what I mean. I thought you moved away."

Patty smiled. "I did, silly. I'm back, visiting my aunt and uncle."

Janet turned to Karen. "This is Patty. She used to be in my class. We used to do lots of crazy things together."

"Hi." Karen wanted to be friendly, but there was something about Patty that she didn't like.

Maybe it was the way that Patty and Janet were giggling together. Karen didn't see what was so funny all of a sudden.

Janet stood up. "Patty and I are going in for another swim," she told Karen. "We're going past that white marker, so maybe you'd better not come."

Karen dug her toe into the sand. "All right. I'll wait here."

Karen stared after the two girls for a minute, then turned to Rosie. "I don't have anything else to do," she said, "so I might as well help you with your sand castle."

Secretly, Karen was proud of the pretty castle Rosie had started. She was beginning to be glad her sister had come along after all. At least Rosie was someone to play with.

Janet and Patty were gone so long that Karen wondered if they were ever coming back. Just when Karen was getting worried that something had happened to them, she saw them walking along the shore, arm in arm.

"I'm going home with Patty," Janet called. "Maybe I'll see you tomorrow."

"Sure, see you around," Karen called back, trying to sound like she didn't care.

"Where did Janet and that other girl go?" Rosie asked.

"Oh, who cares!" Karen blinked back her tears.

Rosie patted her big sister's hand. "That's all right. Now we can work on my sand castle."

"Who wants to work on a dumb old castle!" And with one kick, Karen turned the castle into a messy heap of sand.

Rosie let out a shriek.

"Cut it out," Karen said. "Come on, get your stuff together. We're leaving!"

Several days later, Karen received a phone call.

"Hi, it's me — Janet," said the voice at the other end of the line. "I'm going to the movies this afternoon. Do you want to come?"

Karen was too happy to say a word at first. After that day at the beach, Karen had been positive that Janet didn't want to be friends anymore.

"S-Sure, I'll come. I just have to leave a note for my mother in case she comes home from work early. I won't bring my little sister this time. Rosie's at my grandfather's today."

"Okay, I'll meet you at the theater."

Karen and Janet had no trouble finding good seats once they got to the theater. After the first cartoon, Janet turned to Karen.

"I'm getting some popcorn," she whispered. "Save my place."

By the time the next cartoon started, Janet still hadn't come back.

I'd better go look for her, thought Karen. *Maybe she got lost.*

Karen couldn't find Janet at the counter where the food was sold.

She must have gone back to our seats already, Karen thought to herself. *I'll buy us some grape drink. Popcorn makes us thirsty.*

Karen bought two drinks and started to go back to her seat. As she walked past the last row, something hit her in the neck.

Karen looked over and saw that some kids were throwing popcorn at everyone who walked by. Then she noticed that it was Janet sitting with some of her classmates.

"Hey, Janet," whispered Karen. "Where were you? Did you get lost?"

"No, I just wanted to sit here instead."

Karen started to sit down in the seat next to Janet. A boy threw his arm across that chair.

"This row is for fourth graders," he told Karen. "Are you in the fourth grade?"

"No, but —"

"Then you can't sit here. Go sit with the little kids where you belong!"

Karen looked at Janet, but Janet didn't say anything. She just laughed along with the others.

Karen was so angry that she was shaking. She couldn't think of anything to say, so she leaned over and poured grape drink all over Janet's head. Then, as Janet sputtered and choked, Karen ran out of the theater.

That night, Karen was feeding her turtle when her mother came into her room.

"Janet Wilson's mother called. She told me what happened today. She said Janet's clothes are a mess."

Karen stared at the floor. "I just had to get back at her," she mumbled.

"For what?"

With tears in her eyes, Karen told her everything that had happened at the movies. While she was talking, Rosie popped her head in the doorway.

"Janet left Karen alone at the beach too," said Rosie. "That's when Karen kicked down my sand castle."

"Tattletale," said Karen.

"Is that true?" asked her mother.

Karen nodded. "I don't know how to explain it, Mom. Sometimes I get so mad that I just have to *do* something!"

Karen's mother sat down. "It's all right to get mad, and it's all right to do something about it."

"It is?"

"Sure, but you can't do just anything."

Karen thought for a minute. "You're right. Maybe I should have hit her."

"You know that's no good," said her mother. "When people make you angry, you should try telling them that. They might not even know you're angry."

"Really?" asked Karen. "Do you think it's too late to tell Janet?"

"That's up to you," her mother answered.

The next morning, Karen knocked on Janet's door. Janet opened it a crack.

"What do you want? Did you come over to pour more grape drink on my head?"

Karen gulped. "I came over to tell you I'm sorry I did that. I . . . I was really mad at you, though."

Janet opened the door wider. "Why were you mad?"

"Because you asked me to the movies and then you wouldn't sit with me. You left me alone when we went to the beach too."

Janet came out onto the porch. "I guess that was kind of mean. I just wasn't thinking about how you'd feel."

Karen started down the stairs. "That's all I wanted to say. Oh, and I'm glad the grape drink didn't turn your hair purple."

"Wait," called Janet. "There's a new slide at the playground. It's really scary. Do you want to go?"

Karen turned around. "Sure —" she started to say, then stopped. "I can't. I just remembered — Rosie's building a playhouse today and she asked me to help. Even though she's just a little kid, she likes me a lot and we have fun together."

"Okay," said Janet. "How about tomorrow?"

"Sure thing," Karen called, and she skipped down the street.

West Goshen School Library

GOSHEN COMMUNITY SCHOOLS   WG9
FIC HOG
Hogan, Paula Z.
Sometimes I get so mad /

3 3381 00047 0679

WITHDRAWN

F   **Hogan, Paula Z**
Hog   Sometimes I get so mad; illus. by Karen Shapiro. Raintree
        © 1980

9-80   31p   illus
4535
        Karen learns to deal with anger directly and positively, instead of
in passive and negative ways.

        1. Anger-Fiction   I. Title

                                                        E/Fic